# DIAMOND HEIST

## The Shadow Within

### VOLUME II

Dr. Maxwell Shimba

Shimba Publishing, LLC.

Printed by Shimba Publishing LLC
Printed in the United States of America

# TABLE OF CONTENTS

# INTRODUCTION

Volume II: The Shadows Within

In this next installment, The Shadows Within, the stakes are raised as Dr. Maxwell Shimba, an esteemed theologian and author, enters the scene with an unexpected twist. A package arrives from overseas, containing an exquisite and rare diamond – a gift from an anonymous admirer of his work, or so he believes. But the arrival of this diamond thrusts Dr. Shimba into the world of 47th Street's underbelly, where the glamorous façade of New York's Diamond District hides a ruthless network of scammers, thieves, and desperate players willing to do anything for a piece of the prize.

As Dr. Shimba unwittingly becomes a target, Detectives James Walker and Sarah Martinez are pulled back into the chaos. Their prior investigation into the Diamond Heist left a power vacuum that only intensified the crime on 47th Street, and now they're facing a new surge of illicit activity driven by the scramble for Dr. Shimba's diamond.

The detectives quickly realize that this is no ordinary package; it's a catalyst, sparking renewed interest from Marcus Kane's old allies, shadowy figures who lurk in the city's hidden corners, each with their own stake in the game.

Dr. Shimba, known more for his quiet intellectual pursuits than the rough world of high-stakes crime, must now navigate an environment where trust is currency, and betrayal is expected. As he tries to safeguard the diamond and uncover the intentions behind its mysterious arrival, he finds himself at odds with a world he never intended to enter. His dedication to truth and integrity will be tested as he comes face-to-face with criminals who view his kindness as weakness and his wealth of knowledge as leverage.

Meanwhile, Walker and Martinez dive deeper into the criminal web woven around Dr. Shimba. Their investigation reveals a new, sophisticated network operating on 47th Street, one that extends beyond the usual suspects. A group of elite scammers, known as "The Shadows," has emerged, specializing in deception, forgery, and intimidation to exploit valuable assets. As the detectives follow the leads, they uncover that "The Shadows" have been watching Dr. Shimba for weeks, planning a con that would strip him not only of his diamond but of his reputation and financial stability.

As the volume unfolds, Dr. Shimba finds allies in unexpected places, including figures from his own religious community, who rally to support him as he faces threats both subtle and overt. With each new twist, he uncovers pieces of a puzzle pointing to something far bigger than a single diamond – a conspiracy involving high-profile figures and international crime rings. As Walker and Martinez race against time to protect him, Dr. Shimba must learn to balance his faith and moral values with the harsh realities of the Diamond District's criminal underworld.

The Shadows Within is an intricate tale of deception, resilience, and unexpected alliances, where Dr. Shimba's resolve and intelligence are put to the ultimate test. With danger closing in from every side, he, along with Walker and Martinez, will confront the darker side of ambition and greed in a relentless battle to preserve his legacy, his life, and his ideals. The journey into the heart of New York's most hidden secrets has only just begun, and as Dr. Shimba soon realizes, the shadows of 47th Street run far deeper than he could have ever imagined.

# DR. MAXWELL SHIMBA

# CHAPTER 01

---

**THE ARRIVAL**

A brisk, chilly wind swept through New York City's Diamond District as Dr. Maxwell Shimba stepped out of his apartment, a morning coffee in hand, and hailed a taxi to his office. The city was buzzing with its usual energy, but as he glanced down at his watch, he couldn't shake a slight unease that had followed him since the night before. An unusual package from an unknown sender had arrived on his doorstep, a small, sleek box with no note or return address. Inside was a diamond, unlike anything he had ever seen— radiant, flawless, and strangely hypnotic.

As a theologian and academic, Dr. Shimba's life revolved around books and manuscripts, not the intrigue of New York's diamond trade. He had little interest in gemstones, yet this diamond's origin piqued his curiosity. Had it been sent by a supporter, an admirer of his work? Or, perhaps, it was a gift from a museum he'd consulted on an ancient artifact study last year. But why the mystery? The more he examined the diamond, the less sense it made. It was valuable beyond reason and would undoubtedly attract unwanted attention if anyone found out.

Lost in thought, he didn't notice the pair of eyes watching him as he entered his office building on Madison Avenue. In the shadows across the street, two men in dark jackets exchanged glances and muttered to one another before slipping into an unmarked black car. They had been watching Dr. Shimba for several days, tracking his every move. They knew about the diamond, and they weren't the only ones. News had already spread in certain circles that the diamond was worth millions, a prize too tempting for New York's most cunning criminals to ignore.

Meanwhile, detectives James Walker and Sarah Martinez were at the precinct, buried in a mountain of reports on the latest string of diamond thefts that had hit 47th Street. Each heist was executed with precision, almost militaristic in its planning. The clues pointed to a new wave of scammers, and whispers of "The Shadows," an elite network of con artists, had become commonplace on the street. Walker and Martinez had been following leads for weeks, but each time they got close, the trail went cold. Little did they know, their next major case was about to land right on their doorstep.

As Dr. Shimba settled in for the morning, he reached out to his assistant to begin his research for a new lecture series. But the diamond lingered in his mind, its presence both fascinating and unsettling. Finally, he decided to reach out to a trusted colleague with ties to the diamond industry. Maybe, just maybe, they could shed some light on what he was holding and who might have sent it. But before he could make the call, a knock sounded at his door, and two men in suits introduced themselves as associates from a "private security firm" with an interest in rare gemstones.

They handed him their cards, thinly veiled expressions of concern plastered across their faces. Dr. Shimba felt a sudden rush of adrenaline; he knew enough to sense that something was off. The men claimed they wanted to ensure his "asset" remained safe in the turbulent world of the Diamond District, hinting that others may already be after it. With a polite smile and a firm handshake, Dr. Shimba sent them on their way, their cards slipping into his desk drawer. As they departed, he watched them through his window, realizing he'd just stepped into a game he neither understood nor wanted to play. But the die had been cast, and as he turned back to his desk, a single thought weighed on him: the shadows had already found him.

# CHAPTER 02

---

**THE WARNING**

The following morning, Dr. Maxwell Shimba found himself at his desk, examining the diamond once more, its light refracting through the early sun that filtered in through his office window. The diamond was mesmerizing, flawless in a way that almost seemed unnatural. But it wasn't just the beauty of the stone that kept him enthralled—it was the mystery that surrounded it. The sense of something looming unsettled him, but as a man of reason and faith, he was determined to unravel the puzzle logically, starting with an inquiry into the diamond's origins.

The day's work was abruptly interrupted by his phone ringing, the name "Detective James Walker" flashing on the screen. Dr. Shimba had known Walker for years, their paths crossing during a lecture Dr. Shimba gave on ethics in law enforcement. Walker was a no-nonsense detective, known for his dedication to the truth and his sharp instincts. Intrigued by the timing, Dr. Shimba answered, hearing Walker's familiar voice on the other end.

"Dr. Shimba," Walker began, his tone immediately serious. "I need to talk to you. It's about the diamond. Word's out on the street, and it's not good news."

As the detective outlined what he'd learned, Dr. Shimba listened in silence, growing more concerned with every word. Walker explained that several crime circles, including a dangerous group known as "The Shadows," had caught wind of the diamond's arrival. They were infamous for their scams and thefts in the Diamond District, a covert ring that specialized in prying valuable stones from their unsuspecting owners using elaborate tricks and threats. "These guys don't back down easily," Walker warned. "If they've set their sights on you, they won't stop until they get what they want."

Walker's concern wasn't merely professional—it was personal. As soon as he'd heard about Dr. Shimba's new acquisition, he'd known trouble would follow. He urged Dr.

Shimba to consider handing over the diamond to the authorities for safekeeping. But Dr. Shimba hesitated; the mystery and the intention behind this gift meant something to him, and he wasn't ready to relinquish it until he understood its full story. He promised Walker he'd be cautious, sensing his friend's frustration but respecting his own intuition.

Later that day, Dr. Shimba decided to take a detour through the Diamond District on his way home, seeking answers from some of the dealers he knew. The busy sidewalks were teeming with people, the street glimmering with storefronts displaying everything from modest jewelry to dazzling multi-carat diamonds. But as he walked, he couldn't shake the feeling of being watched, a shadow that seemed to follow him around every corner.

Back at his apartment that night, a sleek black envelope awaited him. Inside, written in precise handwriting, was a simple message: "Give us the diamond, and this ends here." The note was unsigned, but the threat was clear. As Dr. Shimba stared at the words, he felt a weight settle over him. The shadows were closing in, and he was now part of a dangerous game, one that wouldn't end until he surrendered or discovered the truth.

# CHAPTER 03

---

## INTO THE SHADOWS

Dr. Maxwell Shimba sat in his dimly lit apartment, staring at the note from "The Shadows" and feeling the walls close in around him. The message was chillingly direct, each word laced with an unspoken threat. The diamond on his desk sparkled innocently, a stark contrast to the danger it had brought into his life. He knew he couldn't handle this alone, but he wasn't ready to surrender the diamond or retreat from the mystery just yet. Driven by a combination of curiosity and resolve, he made up his mind—he would seek answers himself.

The next morning, Dr. Shimba reached out to Detective Sarah Martinez, Walker's sharp-witted partner who had a reputation for cutting through layers of deceit. Sarah had a gift for reading between the lines and a determination that matched Walker's. Over coffee at a quiet café near his apartment, he explained the situation, showing her the diamond and the threatening note. She examined the stone carefully, holding it up to the light, her expression thoughtful. "You realize," she said finally, "that if The Shadows know about this diamond, they've likely been watching you for weeks. They're patient, and they don't miss a single detail."

Sarah suggested they take the diamond to an expert she trusted, a reclusive but brilliant gemologist named Leo Faulkner, who had a knack for uncovering hidden histories behind stones. He operated from an unmarked office on the outskirts of Manhattan, a place where only trusted clients were allowed. If there was something unusual about this diamond, Leo would find it.

Later that day, Dr. Shimba and Sarah visited Leo's office. The walls were lined with rare stones and artifacts from around the world, each piece meticulously cataloged. Leo, a middle-aged man with a keen gaze and a reserved demeanor, took the diamond in hand, examining it under various lenses and lights, his face a mask of concentration. After a few silent minutes, he looked up, his eyes sharp. "This isn't just any diamond," he said. "It's part of the 'Firestorm Collection'—a set of legendary stones said to be cursed. Each one is flawless, rare beyond belief, and tied to a legacy of theft, betrayal, and mystery. No one knows who owns the full collection, but rumors say it has changed hands many times in shadowy, dangerous circles."

Dr. Shimba felt a chill. He'd expected something valuable, but this? A cursed gem tied to a legacy of intrigue? Sarah's face grew serious as Leo continued, "If The Shadows are after this, they're not the only ones. There's another player in the game—a collector known as 'The Broker.' No one knows his real identity, but he deals exclusively in artifacts with dubious histories. He'd pay millions for this, and he has a network even The Shadows fear."

The pieces were falling into place, but this newfound knowledge brought Dr. Shimba no comfort. He thanked Leo and pocketed the diamond, feeling its weight more heavily than ever. Sarah warned him that things would only intensify from here. The Shadows wouldn't stop, and now that he knew the diamond's significance, others would try to silence him. The deeper he went, the fewer friends he would have, and she urged him to consider letting the police take over.

As they left the office, a sleek black car pulled up to the curb, the driver's tinted window rolling down just enough to reveal a figure in a dark suit. "Dr. Shimba," the figure said with a faint, unsettling smile. "It's time we had a chat." The voice was smooth, confident, and vaguely familiar, yet Dr. Shimba couldn't place it. The stranger gestured for him to enter the car, and as Sarah moved forward to intervene, two more men stepped out, blocking her path. Her hand went instinctively to her sidearm, but the stranger held up his hand, signaling for peace.

"Let's not escalate things," he said calmly. "I simply want a word with the good doctor. You have my word that no harm will come to him. Yet."

With a reluctant nod, Dr. Shimba stepped forward, a mix of dread and curiosity propelling him. He climbed into the car, and as the door closed behind him, the car pulled away, leaving Sarah standing on the curb, tension in her every muscle. She watched as it disappeared into the traffic, her mind racing for a plan.

Inside the car, the figure turned to face Dr. Shimba, his gaze intense and unnerving. "You've gotten yourself into something far bigger than you realize, Dr. Shimba," he said. "Allow me to introduce myself—I am The Broker."

# CHAPTER 04

---

## THE BROKER'S OFFER

The city lights blurred past the tinted windows as Dr. Shimba found himself alone with The Broker, the elusive figure whose influence extended far beyond New York's borders. The man was impeccably dressed, his suit tailored to perfection, with a presence that was both sophisticated and ominous. His eyes, sharp and calculating, studied Dr. Shimba with an unsettling intensity. As the car weaved through the city streets, Dr. Shimba's unease grew, yet his curiosity outweighed his fear.

"Dr. Shimba," The Broker began, his voice smooth and measured, "you are in possession of something that does not belong to you. This diamond—while beautiful—is far more than a mere gem. It's a piece of history, a symbol of wealth and power that carries with it a dangerous legacy. I trust that by now, you know a bit about the 'Firestorm Collection'?"

Dr. Shimba nodded, his mind racing. "I've heard that it's a collection of flawless, rare stones with a history of theft and betrayal. But why was it sent to me? I'm not involved in the diamond industry."

The Broker smiled faintly, as if amused by Shimba's naivete. "Perhaps it was a test, Dr. Shimba. Or perhaps someone wanted you involved precisely because you are an outsider, someone with credibility and intelligence. You may not understand the diamond's history, but it was meant to draw you into this world, where power and deception are everything. Whoever sent it to you intended for it to shake up the underworld—and it has done precisely that."

He paused, letting his words sink in before continuing. "But here's the truth, Dr. Shimba. I am offering you a way out. Hand over the diamond, and I will ensure that you are left alone. The Shadows and their associates won't bother you.

They answer to me, and I can make this all disappear with a simple word."

Dr. Shimba hesitated, his mind struggling to process the weight of The Broker's offer. He had no desire to be drawn into a world of crime and secrecy, yet a part of him felt compelled to understand why he had been chosen to receive this mysterious gem. He looked directly at The Broker, meeting his steely gaze. "And what do you intend to do with it?"

The Broker chuckled softly, his tone calm but authoritative. "The diamond belongs with the rest of the Firestorm Collection. I have spent years acquiring each piece, tracking them down across continents, prying them from the hands of collectors and criminals alike. With this final stone, the collection will be complete, and I will possess something that no one else in the world can claim. It's not about wealth, Dr. Shimba. It's about legacy. Power. Control over the rarest and most valuable artifacts in existence."

Dr. Shimba felt a chill run through him. The Broker's ambition was clear, and he understood now that this man's power extended far beyond anything he could have imagined. Returning the diamond would indeed free him from this nightmare, but it would also allow The Broker to achieve his goal, consolidating the collection's power and influence in his hands.

"I need time to think," Dr. Shimba said finally, his voice steady. "This diamond didn't come into my possession by accident. There's a reason it was sent to me, and I need to understand that reason before I make any decisions."

The Broker's face darkened slightly, his patience visibly tested, but he nodded. "Very well, Dr. Shimba. But understand this: time is not on your side. There are others who seek this diamond, and they are not bound by the same civility that I am. The Shadows will grow restless, and others will come knocking—if you choose to keep the stone, you will invite chaos into your life."

The car slowed to a stop in front of Dr. Shimba's apartment building. As the door opened, The Broker leaned forward, his gaze penetrating. "You have forty-eight hours. Make your choice wisely. Once the clock runs out, I cannot guarantee your safety."

Dr. Shimba stepped out, the weight of the decision pressing down on him. As the car pulled away, he glanced up at his building, each window casting a ghostly reflection in the darkening sky. He was back home, yet he felt like he was teetering on the edge of something far darker than he had anticipated.

Inside, he paced his living room, turning the diamond over in his hand, its brilliance casting tiny prisms on the walls.

He knew he was entangled in a web of greed, history, and danger. The Broker's warning echoed in his mind: Forty-eight hours.

For a long moment, he stood in silence, his decision not yet clear. Then, a new resolve took root within him. This was more than a simple trade. It was a test of his courage, his principles, and his quest for the truth. Dr. Shimba was no criminal, but he was a man of conviction, and he would not be swayed by power or intimidation. The mystery of the diamond—and its dark legacy—would not be surrendered so easily.

# CHAPTER 05

**ALLIES AND ENEMIES**

Dr. Shimba couldn't shake the feeling of eyes on him as he returned to his apartment. The weight of The Broker's ultimatum pressed heavily on his mind. He knew he had two days, but he also knew that forty-eight hours in a world of crime and secrecy could vanish in the blink of an eye. To move forward, he needed allies who were skilled, trustworthy, and familiar with New York's hidden networks.

His first call was to Detective Sarah Martinez. She picked up immediately, her voice calm but edged with concern. "Maxwell, you're back. Did you find anything out?"

"Yes, but it's worse than I imagined," he replied, his voice barely above a whisper. "There's someone called The Broker. He's… a collector with a ruthless reputation. He wants the diamond, and he's given me forty-eight hours to hand it over."

There was a pause on the line, and he could hear her take a deep breath. "The Broker? I've heard of him. He's involved in art, relics, diamonds—anything rare and valuable. If he's in the game, then you're dealing with more than just street criminals. This is serious, Maxwell."

"I know, Sarah. I didn't know where else to turn," he admitted. "But I don't plan on handing it over to him just yet. There's a reason this diamond came to me, and I need to understand why."

Sarah's tone softened. "You don't have to face this alone, Maxwell. I'll be there in fifteen minutes."

True to her word, Sarah arrived swiftly, and they mapped out a plan. She suggested reaching out to Detective James Walker, her partner and a seasoned NYPD investigator known for his resourcefulness and connections in the city. Walker had contacts on every street corner and could provide insight into The Broker's operations and whereabouts. Though Walker often preferred to work solo, he trusted Sarah's instincts and her dedication to justice.

After a brief phone call, Walker agreed to meet them at an old speakeasy in Lower Manhattan that he often used for confidential meetings. The dimly lit venue was perfect for discretion, and within an hour, the three were gathered in a private booth, surrounded by the low hum of jazz and muted conversations.

Walker got straight to the point, his voice a low murmur. "The Broker is a ghost, Shimba. No fingerprints, no trail. He's untouchable. But there's one person who may know more—his right-hand woman, Cassandra 'Cassie' Monroe. She's as clever as she is dangerous, and she's known to manage a lot of his transactions. If anyone knows what The Broker's plans are, it's her."

Sarah's eyebrows shot up. "Cassie? You think she'll talk?"

Walker gave a grim nod. "If she has something to gain, maybe. She's always looking for leverage, and it's rumored she and The Broker don't always see eye-to-eye. She might have her own reasons for wanting to see him fail."

Dr. Shimba considered this. The idea of meeting Cassie was risky, but if she held even a fraction of the information he needed, it could shift the balance in his favor. And with only forty-eight hours left, time wasn't on his side.

"Can you set it up?" Dr. Shimba asked.

Walker's jaw tightened. "I can try, but she won't meet just anyone. And if The Broker finds out, he'll know exactly who she's been talking to."

After a few minutes of silent deliberation, Walker made the call, reaching out to a contact in Cassie's circle. There was no guarantee she would agree, but the message was passed along. They would meet in the same speakeasy in two hours if she accepted.

As they waited, the tension was palpable. Every passerby looked like a potential spy, and every clink of glass felt like a signal. Finally, just as the clock approached midnight, Cassie Monroe walked in. Tall and striking, with sharp eyes and an air of defiance, she scanned the room before heading to their booth. She was dressed in dark, understated elegance, exuding an aura that was as magnetic as it was dangerous.

"So, you're the infamous Dr. Shimba," she said, her voice dripping with sarcasm as she slid into the booth. Her gaze flickered to Walker and Sarah, acknowledging them with a barely perceptible nod before focusing back on Shimba. "I have to say, you don't look like someone who'd be tangled up with a piece from the Firestorm Collection."

Shimba met her gaze, choosing his words carefully. "This diamond found its way to me, Cassie. And now, The

Broker wants it back. I just want to know why. What's so important about completing the collection?"

Cassie's eyes narrowed, and she leaned back, as if weighing how much to reveal. "The Firestorm Collection isn't just a set of diamonds, Dr. Shimba. It's a symbol. Each stone was once owned by a legendary figure, passed down through the ages. Together, they represent the ultimate status, a kind of unspoken royalty in the underworld. Whoever holds the full collection holds influence, loyalty, and fear."

Walker interrupted, leaning forward. "And what does The Broker plan to do with it?"

Cassie shrugged nonchalantly. "Control, Detective. He doesn't care about the stones' beauty or value. He wants what they represent. But…" Her gaze shifted to Shimba, a flicker of intrigue in her eyes. "I suspect there's more to this than he's letting on. Why else would he be so desperate to track down a single stone?"

Dr. Shimba's pulse quickened. He knew Cassie was holding back, but there was a hint in her expression, a silent invitation. She was as entangled in this as he was, though her motivations were still unclear.

Cassie looked him over, her lips curving in a faint smile. "Maybe you're more than an accidental player in all this, Dr. Shimba. If you're serious about finding answers, I could use an ally who isn't bound by the rules of the game. But it won't be safe, and once you're in, there's no turning back."

Dr. Shimba felt a chill as her words settled over him. He was on the verge of stepping even deeper into a world of deception and betrayal, a world he barely understood. But if Cassie was right, if there was more to this diamond than even The Broker understood, then he couldn't walk away.

He extended his hand across the table. "Then let's find out what he's hiding."

Cassie's grip was firm as she shook his hand, sealing a fragile alliance. Walker and Sarah exchanged uneasy glances, aware that this decision had placed Shimba on an irrevocable path. The Broker's forty-eight-hour deadline was ticking, and with Cassie by their side, they had one shot to uncover the truth—before The Broker closed in.

# CHAPTER 06

**BENEATH THE SURFACE**

The alliance with Cassie added an electric edge to their team. As the night deepened, the four of them—Dr. Shimba, Detective Walker, Detective Martinez, and Cassie—gathered around a dimly lit table, maps and documents spread before them. Their voices were low, mingling with the whispers of jazz from a distant speaker, while the streets outside held a restless energy.

Cassie leaned over the table, pointing at a series of addresses scrawled in her precise handwriting. "If we're going to figure out what The Broker's really after, we need to understand his network. He doesn't just hold power through the Firestorm Collection; he's tied into hidden vaults, safehouses, and private transactions all over the city."

Walker's eyes scanned the map, tracing the lines she'd marked. "I recognize some of these locations—East Village, the Upper West Side, and one down in Tribeca. These aren't just random spots, are they?"

Cassie smirked. "Not at all. Each one is a nexus for The Broker's influence. The Tribeca location, for instance, is an old bank that was converted into a private vault. Rumor has it he keeps pieces of his collection there, along with other valuables. That's our first lead."

Dr. Shimba felt the weight of the task ahead of them. Breaking into one of The Broker's vaults was dangerous; if they were caught, they'd be lucky to leave alive. But Cassie's confidence, her deep knowledge of The Broker's inner workings, gave them a unique advantage. And time was slipping away.

"So, we go to the Tribeca vault first," he said, his tone resolute. "But how do we get in? And how do we do it without alerting his people?"

Cassie's gaze held a glint of excitement. "Leave that part to me. I've infiltrated it once before, a few years back, before he tightened his security. The vault's entrance is under a defunct art gallery. It's unassuming, but inside, there's a hidden elevator that takes you down to a secure basement. I'll handle the locks and codes; you three need to be my eyes and ears."

Walker leaned back, crossing his arms with a look of concern. "And if he's increased security since you were last there?"Cassie shrugged. "Then we improvise. But if we're quick and quiet, we'll be in and out before anyone knows we're there."

As the plan took shape, they prepared themselves mentally for what lay ahead. Cassie left to gather her gear, and Dr. Shimba, Walker, and Sarah took a moment to steel their nerves.

Late that night, they met outside the darkened art gallery in Tribeca. The street was empty, shrouded in shadows as a light drizzle began to fall. Cassie led the way, pulling open a side door with a gloved hand. She moved like a shadow herself, her footsteps silent, her expression focused. They followed her inside, moving through a narrow corridor lined with dusty paintings and sculptures.

At the end of the hallway, they reached a plain door, behind which lay the hidden elevator. Cassie knelt, pulling a slim toolkit from her bag. Within seconds, the lock clicked open, and she motioned for them to enter.

The elevator creaked as it descended, carrying them deeper beneath the city. When the doors opened, they stepped into a long, dimly lit corridor. Cassie pointed to the far end, where a reinforced metal door awaited them.

"This is it," she whispered, moving with practiced precision as she keyed in a series of codes. The door slid open with a soft hiss, revealing the vault's interior.

Rows of reinforced cabinets lined the walls, each with a code-locked panel. Cassie moved with purpose, scanning each cabinet until she found one labeled with a subtle, engraved emblem—a firestorm insignia, hidden in plain sight.

"This is the one," she murmured, inputting another code. When the door clicked open, Dr. Shimba stepped forward, his breath catching at the sight inside.

There, resting on a velvet cloth, was another diamond from the Firestorm Collection. Unlike the one he had, this stone was larger, its surface a deep blue that seemed to hold mysteries of its own. But it wasn't just the diamond that drew his attention. Next to it lay a small notebook, its leather cover worn and scrawled with symbols.

Sarah reached for it, flipping through the pages. Her eyes widened as she scanned the handwritten notes. "This is a ledger of transactions… buyers, sellers, dates. And here—" She pointed to a passage. "This diamond wasn't the last. The Broker has been searching for years, and there are still a few pieces left unclaimed."

Cassie glanced over her shoulder, a satisfied smirk on her face. "That's what he doesn't want anyone to know. He's not as powerful as he pretends. He needs those last pieces to complete his grip on the collection. Without them, he's vulnerable."

Walker frowned. "So, the diamond Dr. Shimba has—it's critical to his entire plan."

Dr. Shimba looked down at the blue diamond, a wave of realization hitting him. "He needs both of these to complete the set. Without them, his entire collection remains incomplete. It's symbolic, a fractured crown."

Cassie closed the cabinet door and locked it, her voice sharp. "Now we know his weakness. But we need to get out of here before someone notices."

Just as they turned to leave, a faint noise echoed down the corridor—the sound of approaching footsteps. Cassie froze, exchanging a tense look with Walker. "We're not alone."

They moved quickly but quietly back toward the elevator. The footsteps grew louder, heavy and purposeful. As they reached the elevator, Cassie jabbed the button, willing the doors to open faster.

The elevator door slid open, and they piled inside, hearts pounding as they ascended. Just as the doors closed, a shadowy figure rounded the corner, their gaze locking onto the retreating group. They heard a muffled curse from the other side just as the elevator began to rise, taking them back to street level.

They spilled out into the night, adrenaline still coursing through their veins as they quickly left the scene. Back on the street, they regrouped at a nearby diner, each of them catching their breath as they processed the discovery.

"We have leverage now," Sarah said, clutching the notebook tightly. "This is more than he wanted anyone to know. We've got proof that he's vulnerable."

Dr. Shimba nodded, determination hardening his resolve. "This changes everything. We're not just players in his game anymore. We have a chance to take control."

Cassie gave him an approving nod, a new respect in her eyes. "Then let's make him sweat. We'll use this information to draw him out, to finally understand why he's obsessed with these stones."

As they sat in the dim diner, a strange sense of unity settled over the group. They were from different worlds, brought together by chance and necessity, but now they shared a singular purpose. They were no longer just avoiding The Broker; they were preparing to confront him, to unmask his intentions and reveal the truth.

But they all knew that this move would only escalate the stakes. The Broker wouldn't back down without a fight, and they'd need every ounce of cunning and courage to see their plan through.

The shadows of New York were vast, and they'd barely begun to navigate the depths. But with every discovery, they moved closer to exposing the real story behind the Firestorm Collection—and the mysterious forces pulling the strings from within.

# CHAPTER 07

## THE TRAP TIGHTENS

The diner buzzed with muted conversations, but at their booth, an intense silence hung in the air. Detective Walker's gaze was sharp as he scanned the notes Sarah had pulled from The Broker's ledger. Each entry seemed to tighten the invisible noose around them, a record of dirty deals, bribes, and high-stakes trades that fed The Broker's empire. And yet, something in the ledger felt... off. Dr. Shimba leaned in, his finger tracing the pages, before finally raising an eyebrow.

"Do you notice it too?" he asked, his voice low. "Some of these entries are encrypted differently."

Cassie squinted, tilting the notebook towards the dim light. "These aren't just names and dates—these symbols are placeholders for something else, maybe codenames or hidden locations. The Broker isn't just moving diamonds. He's moving something else, something important enough to hide within his own records."

Walker exhaled slowly. "So, if this isn't just about diamonds, then what are we up against?"

Before they could delve deeper, Dr. Shimba's phone vibrated in his pocket. Frowning, he pulled it out and glanced at the unknown number flashing on the screen. Something in his gut warned him to ignore it, but the curiosity overruled his hesitation. He answered, bringing the phone to his ear cautiously.

A voice, cold and calculated, greeted him. "Dr. Shimba, you've been busy."

The unmistakable chill of The Broker's voice sent a shiver through him. Walker and Sarah leaned closer, their eyes narrowing as they tried to catch every word.

"I see you've found my ledger," The Broker continued. "I warned you, Doctor. But it seems you're intent on making yourself my enemy."

Dr. Shimba's knuckles whitened as he gripped the phone. "If you know where we are, come for me yourself. Stop hiding behind your schemes."

A low chuckle rumbled on the other end. "You're bold, Doctor, I'll give you that. But you're in over your head. If you think that ledger will give you leverage over me, you're sadly mistaken. I know your every move, your every hiding place."

Before Dr. Shimba could respond, a text pinged onto Walker's phone. His face paled as he opened it and handed the screen to Sarah. It was a photo of all four of them, taken just minutes earlier as they sat in the diner.

The realization hit them like a ton of bricks—they were being watched. Dr. Shimba glanced around the diner, his eyes darting over every corner, every figure, but everyone looked engrossed in their own worlds, oblivious to the invisible threat that loomed over them.

The Broker continued, his voice laced with dark amusement. "I have eyes everywhere, Doctor. I suggest you return what you took, or you'll find out how quickly I can make good on my promises."

The line went dead, leaving Dr. Shimba gripping the phone in stunned silence. Cassie looked equally shaken, her previous confidence slipping as she scanned the diners around them.

"We've been compromised," she muttered. "He knows too much."

Walker clenched his jaw. "We're sitting ducks here. We need to move."

They left the diner in tense silence, slipping into the night with only the dim streetlights to guide them. Cassie led them down a maze of side streets, her instincts kicking in as she mapped out the safest route. They kept to the shadows, trying to outmaneuver whoever was watching.

As they rounded a corner, Sarah caught sight of a reflection—a figure following them, barely visible in the darkened glass of a storefront. She nudged Walker, signaling for him to notice, and he gave a subtle nod.

"Keep moving," he murmured to the others. "I'll handle this."

Walker slowed his pace, letting the others drift ahead, then slipped into the shadows, waiting. The figure continued, unaware that Walker had doubled back. In one swift move, Walker grabbed the man, pulling him into an alley. The man struggled, but Walker's grip was iron-tight as he demanded answers.

"Who sent you? The Broker?"

The man merely sneered, his silence unyielding, but Walker's instincts told him he was onto something. With a quick, practiced movement, Walker reached into the man's pocket and pulled out a small device—an encrypted GPS tracker, blinking ominously.

Meanwhile, as Dr. Shimba and the others moved further down the street, a black SUV pulled up beside them. The back door swung open, and two masked figures emerged, each holding weapons pointed directly at them.

"Get in," one of them barked.

Cassie's hand inched toward her concealed knife, but Sarah shook her head, subtly signaling for them to comply. They were outnumbered and outgunned. Reluctantly, they climbed into the SUV, the door slamming shut behind them. The SUV sped off into the night, leaving Walker behind, his pulse racing as he realized his team had been taken.

In the SUV, the masked figures remained silent as they drove through the city, weaving through deserted streets until they arrived at a nondescript building on the outskirts of Manhattan. The door opened, and they were led into a dimly lit room, where The Broker himself waited, his silhouette sharp and imposing against the flickering lights.

"Welcome," he greeted, his smile devoid of warmth. "I thought it was time we met face-to-face."

Dr. Shimba held his gaze, defiant despite the unease simmering within him. "If you wanted a meeting, you didn't have to send goons."

The Broker smirked. "Where would the fun in that be? Besides, I needed you to understand who holds the real power here."

He gestured to a glass case on the table behind him. Inside was the final diamond of the Firestorm Collection, shimmering with a cold, otherworldly glow. Dr. Shimba's breath caught. He hadn't realized until now that The Broker's plans ran even deeper—this was the ultimate prize, the culmination of every dangerous twist in the labyrinthine path they'd followed.

The Broker's smile widened as he noticed Dr. Shimba's reaction. "Beautiful, isn't it? The last piece of the puzzle."

But as Dr. Shimba's eyes scanned the room, he noticed something unusual. In the shadows, half-hidden behind the case, was a map marked with a pattern of red lines. It was a blueprint, not just of New York, but of high-profile targets spanning across the country. This wasn't just about diamonds anymore. The Broker's plans involved something far bigger—a network of power and influence that would put him at the helm of the city's most untouchable secrets.

"Your obsession with the diamonds is a cover," Dr. Shimba said, his voice steady. "You're building something bigger. This is about control."

The Broker's gaze hardened, the amusement slipping from his face. "You're smarter than I gave you credit for, Doctor. But you've crossed a line, and now I have to make sure you never reach the end of it."

Just then, the sound of an explosion echoed through the building, and the lights flickered wildly. Walker had arrived, his entry as dramatic as ever, with a blast that sent the guards scattering. In the chaos, Cassie slipped her knife from her sleeve, cutting through her restraints, while Sarah lunged for the nearest guard, disarming him with swift precision.

Dr. Shimba seized the moment, grabbing the glass case and pulling it free from the table. In the midst of the confusion, The Broker locked eyes with him, a look of pure rage flashing across his face.

"This isn't over, Doctor," he snarled. "You may have the diamond, but you're still just a pawn in my game."

Dr. Shimba held his gaze, a steely resolve taking hold. "Then let's see who wins, Broker."

As Walker ushered them towards the exit, the sound of sirens filled the air, signaling that their time was up. They bolted into the night, adrenaline fueling their escape, the final piece of the Firestorm Collection now in their possession.

But they all knew this was only the beginning. The Broker's reach extended far beyond the shadows of New York, and now they were caught in his deadly game—a game that would test their every move and force them deeper into the heart of a mystery that could reshape everything they thought they knew.

# CHAPTER 08

---

## THE GREAT ESCAPE

The explosion reverberated through the dimly lit room, shattering the glass case holding the final diamond of the Firestorm Collection. Shards of glass scattered across the floor as Dr. Shimba snatched the diamond from the broken display, the brilliant gem gleaming in his hand. Beside him, Cassie and Sarah had taken down the guards, each move precise and unhesitating.

The Broker, visibly shaken, regained his composure quickly. His eyes flashed with a deadly calm as he pressed a hidden button under the desk. Alarms blared, filling the building with red flashing lights. Within moments, more guards stormed into the room, armed and ready.

"Leaving so soon?" The Broker taunted, his voice carrying above the noise. "You're not getting out that easily."

Dr. Shimba pocketed the diamond, his gaze never wavering from The Broker. "You underestimated us, and that was your first mistake," he said, his tone steely. He signaled to Cassie and Sarah, who fell in line, ready to take on the new wave of guards.

In the hallway outside, Detective Walker was already engaged in a fierce battle with several armed men, his experience evident in each swift, calculated movement. As Dr. Shimba, Sarah, and Cassie joined him, Walker shot a quick glance at the diamond glinting in Dr. Shimba's hand and nodded. Their objective was complete, but they still had to make it out alive.

The group moved with purpose, fighting off guards as they made their way through the maze-like building. Cassie led the way, using her knowledge of the layout to navigate through side exits and hidden corridors. Each step took them closer to freedom, but The Broker's men were relentless, seemingly appearing around every corner.

As they descended a narrow staircase leading to an underground garage, a squad of heavily armed guards blocked their path. Dr. Shimba's mind raced, calculating their options as Sarah reached into her jacket and produced a smoke grenade she had confiscated from one of the guards earlier. With a quick pull of the pin, she tossed it into the center of the group, the smoke filling the confined space and disorienting their pursuers.

"Now!" she shouted, and they burst through the line, taking advantage of the confusion to break past the guards and into the garage.

The garage was dark, save for the headlights of a black van idling near the exit. Inside, a familiar figure sat behind the wheel—Ryan, Cassie's tech-savvy contact who had assisted them from afar. He waved them over urgently, and they piled into the van, barely closing the doors before he floored the accelerator, sending them speeding out of the garage and into the night.

As the van tore down the streets of Manhattan, Dr. Shimba looked over at Ryan, nodding in gratitude. "You came through for us, Ryan. We owe you one."

Ryan grinned, glancing in the rearview mirror at the group. "Don't mention it. Besides, I couldn't let you guys have all the fun."

But as they weaved through the city streets, The Broker's men were already in pursuit. Black SUVs trailed them, headlights flashing as they closed in. Ryan swerved through traffic, pushing the van to its limits, while Cassie and Sarah readied themselves at the rear, preparing to fend off their pursuers.

Walker leaned forward, issuing directions to Ryan. "Take Fifth Avenue and head toward Central Park. We can lose them in the park's side roads."

Ryan nodded, his hands steady on the wheel as he maneuvered the van with expert precision. They entered Central Park, the thick trees and winding roads providing the cover they needed. But The Broker's men were relentless, their SUVs cutting off every path and closing in on them with every turn.

Cassie fired at the tires of the closest SUV, sending it skidding off the road and crashing into a tree. Sarah aimed at another, her shots precise as the second vehicle spun out of control. But even as they thinned the ranks, more SUVs joined the chase, and it was clear that The Broker had deployed every resource he had to stop them.

Just when the situation seemed hopeless, Walker received a message from his NYPD contacts. Backup was en route, and he could hear the faint sounds of police sirens in the distance. The cavalry was coming.

As the first squad cars appeared, The Broker's men hesitated, realizing they were vastly outnumbered. The police quickly intercepted the SUVs, surrounding them and bringing an end to the pursuit. Dr. Shimba and his team watched as officers moved in, handcuffing the remaining guards.

Walker took a deep breath, his tense posture finally relaxing as he turned to the others. "We did it."

The team exchanged weary but triumphant smiles, the weight of their victory sinking in. They had outmaneuvered The Broker, secured the final diamond, and dismantled his network of criminals. But Dr. Shimba knew this was only a temporary reprieve. The Broker was still out there, his reach extending beyond New York, and his desire for revenge was far from extinguished.

As they drove away, Dr. Shimba looked down at the diamond in his hand, its brilliance casting a glow that hinted at both triumph and caution. This wasn't the end—it was only the beginning of a deeper battle in the shadows, one that would test every ounce of courage and resolve they possessed.

For now, however, they could savor their hard-fought victory, knowing they had escaped the clutches of one of New York's most powerful criminal minds. But somewhere in the city, The Broker was already plotting his next move, waiting for the right moment to strike back. And when he did, Dr. Shimba and his team would be ready, prepared to face whatever new challenge awaited them in the dark, twisting underbelly of New York City.

# CHAPTER 09

## A RAT IN THE RANKS

The precinct buzzed with the aftershocks of Dr. Shimba's successful heist escape. Detective James Walker and Sarah Martinez were cautiously optimistic, though their relief was tempered by the knowledge that The Broker was still at large. As they pieced together the operation's aftermath, one troubling question lingered: how had The Broker's men been able to track them so quickly and precisely?

The entire precinct felt like it was under a shadow. Walker sensed eyes on him, whispers dying down whenever he entered the room. Every officer, every desk clerk, every visitor became a potential suspect in his mind. After all, there was one glaring truth they couldn't ignore: someone had tipped off The Broker. But who?

Detective Sarah Martinez's voice snapped Walker back to the present. "James, we need to talk," she said, her tone edged with urgency. She led him into a private meeting room, her gaze darting toward the windows as if even the walls could listen. She closed the door softly, making sure no one could eavesdrop.

"There's been a leak," she whispered, confirming his suspicions. "I looked into the comms logs from last night. Someone sent an encrypted message from within the precinct to a burner phone linked to one of The Broker's known associates. It's internal, James. Someone on the inside tipped him off."

Walker's jaw tightened. "Are you saying there's a snitch in our ranks?"

Sarah's eyes narrowed. "I'm saying there's a rat somewhere in this building. And they're playing for the other side."

The two detectives exchanged a grim look, the gravity of their situation sinking in. If someone in the precinct was secretly aligned with The Broker, their entire investigation could be compromised. It was no longer just a matter of tracking down criminals on the streets; it was now a dangerous game of trust and deception within their own walls.

That night, Walker and Martinez decided to investigate discreetly. They combed through files, combing through recent arrests and any unusual behavior among their colleagues. To keep things under the radar, they split up, each approaching different officers with casual questions, masking their intent behind routine check-ins.

As Walker questioned one of his colleagues, he noticed Detective Miller, one of the newer hires, fidgeting near the break room. Miller's eyes darted nervously, and he kept glancing at his phone as if expecting a message. He avoided Walker's gaze, something that piqued his interest. Walker casually walked over and greeted him, chatting about a recent case before steering the conversation toward the heist.

"Crazy night last night, huh?" Walker said, eyeing Miller carefully. "We got lucky."

Miller forced a laugh. "Yeah, lucky... I, uh, heard you guys barely got out."

Walker watched as Miller's hand shook slightly. "Yeah, thanks to some backup that arrived just in time," Walker replied, leaning in. "But you know, it's funny—the timing of everything. Almost like The Broker knew where we'd be. I mean, we didn't exactly announce it."

Miller's face paled. "Oh, yeah… well, that's, uh, strange. Could be a coincidence, though."

Walker filed Miller's reaction in his mind but kept the conversation light. He knew he couldn't confront him outright without solid evidence, or else he'd tip off the mole. For now, suspicion was all he had.

Later, in the dimly lit surveillance room, Walker and Sarah huddled over security footage, rewinding to the night of the heist. As they zoomed in on the precinct hallway, they caught a glimpse of Miller entering the restricted comms room at an odd hour. The timestamp coincided with the encrypted message Sarah had found.

"There's our guy," Sarah muttered. "We need a way to catch him in the act, though. If we confront him now, he'll just deny it."

Walker nodded. "Let's set a trap. We'll feed some false information, make it look like we're planning a raid, but we'll set the location somewhere completely off The Broker's radar."

The next morning, they executed their plan, discreetly spreading a rumor around the precinct about an imminent raid on a safe house supposedly tied to The Broker. Walker made sure Miller overheard him talking about it to Sarah, slipping in specific details about the time and location. Now, all they could do was wait and see if Miller would take the bait.

As expected, an hour later, an encrypted message was sent from within the precinct to a familiar burner phone. This time, however, they were ready. Walker had arranged for NYPD tech specialists to trace the message in real time, watching as it pinged off cell towers and led directly to The Broker's network.

With the confirmation they needed, Walker and Sarah cornered Miller in the hallway, his face falling as he realized the game was up. He tried to talk his way out, claiming he was just "doing his job" and didn't realize what he'd stumbled into. But when faced with the evidence, he finally cracked, admitting he had been feeding The Broker information in exchange for a cut of the diamonds.

"What's he planning next?" Walker demanded.

Miller hesitated but saw the futility in silence. "He's not done with Dr. Shimba," he confessed. "There's more at stake here than just diamonds. He's going after something bigger—Dr. Shimba's entire operation, his overseas contacts, everything."

The revelation sent a chill down Walker's spine. This wasn't just about the heist anymore. The Broker was targeting Dr. Shimba's entire network, hoping to dismantle it from the inside out.

As Miller was led away in handcuffs, Walker and Sarah shared a look, both knowing that their battle with The Broker had only intensified. Their victory over the mole was just one small piece in a much larger, darker game. With every step they took, The Broker seemed to be two steps ahead, his web of influence far deeper and more intricate than they had ever imagined.

In the shadows of New York, the hunt continued—but now, Walker knew that the fight wasn't just against criminals in the street. It was against an unseen enemy within their own ranks, one that would stop at nothing to bring them all down.

CHAPTER 10

---

## THE BROKER'S ENDGAME

The precinct buzzed with tension. Miller's confession had shocked the entire department, but the revelations he'd provided hinted at a much larger scheme orchestrated by The Broker. Detective Walker and Sarah Martinez felt the weight of the threat hanging over them—this wasn't just a simple heist anymore. The Broker was moving against Dr. Shimba's entire network, and they had no idea how deep it went or how many others were involved.

Dr. Shimba's office was the team's next stop. The normally calm professor was visibly troubled as he reviewed the new information. He paced his office, his eyes darting to the diamond securely tucked into a velvet-lined case on his desk. That gem, part of a priceless overseas collection, was more than just a glittering prize; it was a key to something far bigger—a network of international art, wealth, and power that The Broker clearly intended to exploit.

"Dr. Shimba," Sarah began, breaking the silence, "Miller indicated that The Broker was targeting more than just your diamonds. He hinted at a broader plan. Any ideas what he could be after?"

Dr. Shimba's gaze sharpened. "It's possible he's after a rare piece in my collection—an artifact passed down through generations, believed to have connections to powerful figures across history. But he's already tried to steal it and failed, which means he must have a backup plan."

Walker nodded, the pieces slowly coming together. "If The Broker can't steal it directly, he'll likely try to undermine your reputation or gain control through another route. Maybe by breaking apart your network."

"Which could cripple my entire operation," Shimba muttered, his expression grave. "There's an event tomorrow at the museum—a private auction for some rare artifacts. It's the perfect venue for The Broker to make a move, but we'll be ready."

The next evening, the grand museum hall glittered with chandeliers and the glint of rare jewels and artifacts displayed on polished pedestals. An array of influential figures mingled, exchanging polite conversation under the watchful eye of hired security. Dr. Shimba, dressed in a tailored suit, stood near the centerpiece artifact—a sapphire-studded relic rumored to hold secrets lost to history. The crowd's attention gravitated toward it, but he kept his gaze steady, scanning for any sign of The Broker or his associates.

Detectives Walker and Martinez stood close by, watching every face, every movement in the crowd. They had set up discreet surveillance and were ready for anything.

As the auction began, Shimba's instincts kicked in. Something was off. He couldn't place it, but he felt an unsettling sense of being watched. Just then, his phone vibrated—a message from an unknown number.

"I have eyes on the relic. One wrong move, and it disappears forever. - The Broker"

Dr. Shimba's stomach clenched. He showed the message to Walker, who quickly signaled to Martinez. "He's here," Walker whispered. "Keep your eyes sharp."

Moments later, a figure dressed in a suit stepped to the podium—a museum official announcing the first item for auction. But as he spoke, he glanced at Shimba with an intensity that set Walker on high alert. Martinez gave a subtle nod toward the auctioneer, noticing the subtle bulge under his jacket. A weapon.

The room dimmed slightly as a spotlight focused on the artifact, and the crowd quieted. The auctioneer's hand hovered over a button, his demeanor poised but tense. Suddenly, he pushed the button, and with a hiss, the lights cut out entirely, plunging the hall into darkness.

Panic erupted. Shadows shifted in the dim light as people stumbled back, their voices filling the air with confusion. Walker could make out shapes moving through the chaos—figures in black, their faces obscured. He and Sarah rushed toward the artifact, but The Broker's men had already taken position around it, expertly coordinating to cover every exit.

A glint caught Walker's eye—the flash of a knife slicing through the display's security glass. In the darkness, Dr. Shimba moved with a swiftness that belied his years, his hands darting out to snatch the artifact from the intruder's grasp. But The Broker's men weren't about to give up easily. One of them lunged, and Shimba found himself cornered, outnumbered.

Just then, the emergency lights flickered on, casting a dim glow over the chaos. Walker and Sarah moved in quickly, their weapons drawn. The crowd scattered, allowing the detectives a clear view of The Broker's henchmen—tall, lean, their expressions hidden behind dark shades and impassive masks.

"Drop it!" Walker ordered, his voice slicing through the noise.

The henchmen hesitated, assessing their options. But a new figure emerged from the crowd, calm and composed, his face framed by sharp cheekbones and a steely gaze. The Broker himself, dressed impeccably, offered Walker a sardonic smile.

"I suppose this is the part where you arrest me?" he said smoothly, as if they were in a game he had already won.

Walker didn't flinch. "Hands behind your head. Now."

But The Broker only laughed. "You've been chasing shadows, Detective. This—" he gestured at the artifact in Shimba's hands, "—is just the beginning."

Suddenly, with a swift motion, The Broker's men launched smoke grenades, filling the hall with a thick, choking haze. Walker and Sarah ducked, trying to maintain their line of sight, but visibility vanished in seconds. They could hear footsteps, sense movement, but The Broker and his men were slipping away.

Walker cursed under his breath as he fought through the smoke, his focus fixed on the sounds. He caught a glimpse of The Broker's silhouette near the exit, but by the time he reached it, the man had vanished into the night.

Back at the precinct, Walker, Sarah, and Shimba sat in the interrogation room, reviewing the night's events. They had thwarted an immediate theft, but The Broker's message echoed in Walker's mind: This is just the beginning.

Dr. Shimba placed the relic on the table between them, his gaze somber. "The Broker isn't after just any diamonds or artifacts," he said. "He's after power, influence—things far beyond simple wealth."

Walker clenched his fists. "And we just got a glimpse of how far he's willing to go to get it."

Sarah looked between the two men, her expression resolute. "Then we need to go even further. If he thinks this is only the beginning, he has no idea what we're capable of."

Walker met her gaze, a fire in his eyes. They knew that with every move they made, The Broker was watching, calculating. But he hadn't yet seen the full force of what they could do. The chase was far from over—and this time, Walker was determined to catch him, no matter the cost.

The Broker had lit the match; now they would set the fire.

# CHAPTER 11

## THE MASK BEHIND THE BADGE

Back at the precinct, Detective Walker sifted through the details of the auction night, trying to make sense of The Broker's audacity. The man had slipped through their fingers so many times that Walker could no longer chalk it up to just luck. There was something more — a hidden advantage that gave The Broker his confidence. And a disturbing thought had started to gnaw at the back of his mind: could someone inside the precinct be working with him?

The idea seemed impossible at first. But the more he thought about it, the clearer it became that The Broker's insider knowledge and careful precision weren't something any ordinary criminal could achieve alone. Every time they'd come close, he had vanished like smoke, leaving them scrambling for leads. He knew too much — not just about their strategies but about the precinct itself. Could he actually be part of the force?

Meanwhile, Detective Sarah Martinez had begun her own quiet investigation. She started by tracing connections within the precinct, examining those with access to critical information about their cases. She noticed a pattern in cases that The Broker had manipulated: they were often overseen by a select few officers who were always one step behind him. One name, in particular, kept surfacing, a detective who had been with the force for years, known for his charm and quiet efficiency.

This man, Detective Carson Lynch, had been a mentor to many officers, including Walker. He was the kind of detective everyone looked up to—calm, collected, and fiercely intelligent. Walker could hardly believe Lynch would betray them, but suspicions were growing. And as Martinez dug deeper, she discovered something shocking: a series of financial transactions linked to offshore accounts, amounts too large to ignore, all tied back to Lynch. It wasn't concrete proof, but it was a start.

Confronting Walker with her suspicions, Martinez laid out her findings, her voice steady but tinged with concern. "Walker, this doesn't look like a coincidence. Lynch has access to nearly every case file involving The Broker, and the money trail is too suspicious to ignore."

Walker felt a pang of disbelief. Carson Lynch had been his friend, his mentor. They'd faced down some of the city's worst criminals together, and he couldn't believe the man he'd trusted for years might be involved in this web of corruption. Yet, the facts stared back at him with cold precision. He had no choice but to follow the evidence, no matter where it led.

The two detectives decided to approach the case with extreme caution, understanding that any misstep could blow their cover. They'd have to be meticulous, watching Lynch's every move without letting on. They combed through old case files, and patterns emerged — cases that had been dismissed, suspects who had mysteriously disappeared, all linked to The Broker's operations.

They worked late into the night, piecing together a trail of betrayal that seemed to go back years. But what they uncovered next would shake them to their core.

As dawn broke, they discovered that Lynch wasn't just working with The Broker — he was The Broker. Lynch's clean-cut detective image had been a facade, masking his role as the mastermind behind the city's most sophisticated crime syndicate. His position within the NYPD gave him access to sensitive information, allowing him to manipulate investigations, divert suspicion, and orchestrate heists with ease.

Walker's stomach churned. It was Lynch's knowledge of the system, his insider status, that had made The Broker so untouchable. The clues were there all along, but no one had dared to question the integrity of a decorated detective. His confidence wasn't arrogance; it was a calculated power play, knowing he had everyone under his thumb.

Martinez looked at Walker, her voice barely a whisper. "This changes everything. The entire precinct — they're all pawns in his game."

Now, more than ever, Walker and Martinez had to tread carefully. Exposing Lynch as The Broker would require undeniable evidence, and any misstep would send him deeper underground. But as they prepared to take down a man who had betrayed them all, one thing became clear: this wasn't just about justice. It was personal.

Their discovery would soon shake the NYPD to its foundations, unveiling corruption woven deep within the force itself. The Broker's confidence, his brazen defiance of the law, now made perfect sense — and with that understanding came a terrifying reality. They were no longer facing just a criminal mastermind; they were going up against one of their own.

# CHAPTER 12

---

## A DANGEROUS GAME

Walker and Martinez sat in silence, the weight of their discovery pressing down on them. Lynch — the respected, trusted detective they had worked alongside for years — was The Broker, orchestrating crime and deceit right under their noses. This was a man who knew their methods, their habits, even their strengths and weaknesses. Now, they would need to leverage everything they had, using all their training and cunning to bring him down without him suspecting a thing.

Walker broke the silence. "We need irrefutable proof. Lynch has an entire network at his disposal, and the second he catches on, he'll disappear, or worse… he'll make sure we disappear."

Martinez nodded, her face set with determination. "We're going to have to outsmart him on his own turf. But if we want to take him down, we'll need to hit him where he least expects it."

They quickly formulated a plan. It involved taking drastic measures and enlisting the help of only a few trusted individuals. They couldn't risk involving anyone who might unknowingly tip Lynch off, so they decided to keep their operation as close to the chest as possible. First, they would need access to Lynch's private communications. They suspected he used burner phones, secure lines, and encrypted emails to manage his criminal network. They would have to uncover every hidden link without him catching on.

To gain intel, they called in Detective Jack Rourke, a former tech specialist with the NYPD, who had a reputation for being both brilliant and discreet. Rourke met with them in an abandoned office building late that night, scanning for potential bugs before they spoke.

"Lynch?" Rourke's eyebrows raised as he took in the gravity of what Walker and Martinez were suggesting. "Are you two serious? If this is true, we're dealing with someone who's got everyone wrapped around his finger. Lynch has friends in high places."

Walker clenched his jaw. "We know. That's why we need you. This has to be airtight."

Rourke hesitated, but eventually nodded, his fingers already dancing across his laptop keyboard. "Alright, let's start by finding any signals tied to him. If he's running an operation like this, he'll have to communicate somehow, and I might be able to track it."

After hours of digging, they hit on a lead: an encrypted network Lynch seemed to use to send instructions to his team. It was a complex web of coded messages routed through various IP addresses, almost impossible to trace without leaving tracks. But Rourke, tapping into surveillance archives and records, slowly unraveled the network.

"Here," he whispered, showing them a map of digital points that spread across New York City. "Each of these is a potential location he could be using. If we can narrow it down, we might catch him red-handed."

Walker's eyes narrowed. "Let's cross-reference these locations with previous crime scenes. If we can identify a pattern, we'll know where he's going to strike next."

Over the next few days, they conducted their investigation in secret, careful to avoid Lynch's suspicions. They pieced together a pattern — shipments in and out of the

Diamond District that coincided with the network's activity. And one address kept recurring: an old, abandoned warehouse on the city's outskirts, a place Walker and Martinez knew well from a cold case involving smuggled diamonds that had gone unsolved.

They set up a stakeout, planting small cameras and microphones around the warehouse. Days passed, with Lynch going about his business as if nothing had changed, but then, one evening, a convoy of black SUVs pulled up outside the warehouse. Men with suspiciously discreet bags entered, and soon after, Lynch arrived, dressed as casually as any civilian.

Walker's heart pounded as he watched the monitor, his eyes narrowing. They needed Lynch to incriminate himself, to do something that tied him definitively to The Broker's network. Martinez gripped his arm. "Look," she whispered.

Inside the warehouse, Lynch moved to a table littered with various high-value items, diamonds and gold scattered alongside electronic equipment and encrypted phones. He picked up a radio, and Walker listened as Lynch's voice crackled over the receiver, his calm tone unmistakable.

"Package received. Tell our friend overseas he'll get his shipment on schedule. Increase security on the next delivery, and make sure no one suspects a thing." He clicked off the radio, and for the first time, a slight smirk crossed his face. "They think they're catching up, but we're three moves ahead."

Walker felt a surge of anger but stayed focused. They had what they needed—Lynch, in his own voice, implicating himself in the heist. But they needed one more step to lock him in—a direct connection to the stolen diamonds or Dr. Shimba's prized artifact.

That night, as they watched Lynch and his team pack up the stolen goods, Rourke's voice broke over the receiver. "I've tracked his phone. Lynch's contacts include someone from Dr. Shimba's circle, someone who could be feeding him information about Shimba's collection."

Walker's eyes widened. "Who?"

"A curator from the museum, name's Arthur Dunn. We're talking serious high-level access to Shimba's collection and other sensitive information."

Martinez immediately dialed Dr. Shimba, briefing him on the news. Dr. Shimba was stunned, but he agreed to help by arranging a fake meeting with Arthur Dunn under the guise of a private showing, a trap that would catch both Dunn and Lynch in the act.

The following evening, Shimba led Dunn into the museum's gallery, pretending to show him a set of newly acquired artifacts. Hidden security cameras recorded everything, while Walker, Martinez, and a SWAT team stood by, ready to move.

Minutes later, Lynch arrived, his expression calculating as he walked through the darkened hallways, meeting Dunn with a barely concealed smirk. He had brought a team, their goal clear — they were there to secure the collection, including the artifact that had set this entire scheme in motion. But just as Lynch reached for the display case, Walker's voice echoed over the intercom.

"Game over, Lynch. Hands up, and step away."

Lynch froze, his confident smile slipping as the room filled with the sound of boots and the click of guns. SWAT members surrounded him and his men. Lynch's eyes narrowed as he looked up, meeting Walker's gaze with cold fury.

"You played this well, Walker," Lynch said, his voice calm but venomous. "But you're a fool if you think this ends here. I've got people everywhere. I am this city's shadows."

Walker stepped forward, meeting his old mentor's gaze with steely resolve. "Not anymore. You may know the shadows, but we'll bring every single one of them into the light. This is the end for you, Lynch."

As they led Lynch and his associates out in cuffs, the reality of their victory sank in. They'd uncovered corruption at the highest level, saved Dr. Shimba's collection, and revealed a dark underbelly of deception within their own ranks. But as Walker watched Lynch's unflinching expression, he knew this wasn't over. The network Lynch had built was vast, and there would be others willing to pick up where he left off.

For now, though, Walker and Martinez could rest, knowing they had exposed the truth and held those responsible to account. The Broker's reign was over, but they would be ready for whatever came next.

---

# CHAPTER 13

## THE UNRAVELING

Detective Walker and Martinez huddled over a cluttered table, maps and photos strewn across its surface as they tried to connect the remaining pieces of the intricate puzzle that was Lynch's criminal empire. Just as Walker began to vocalize his thoughts, his phone buzzed insistently on the table, cutting through the tense atmosphere.

"Who is it?" Martinez asked, glancing at the screen.

"Dr. Shimba," Walker replied, his heart racing as he swiped to answer the call. "Dr. Shimba? What's going on?"

"Detective!" Dr. Shimba's voice crackled through the line, laced with urgency and fear. "I need your help. Something strange just happened."

"What's wrong?" Walker demanded, glancing at Martinez, whose eyes widened with concern.

"A black SUV just pulled up outside my office," Dr. Shimba continued, his voice trembling. "It's been idling there for a few minutes now. I don't know who it is or what they want, but they delivered a package — a black box wrapped with a black ribbon. I didn't open it. I'm scared, Walker. What should I do?"

"Stay calm," Walker instructed, his mind racing. "Lock the door and stay away from the windows. We're on our way."

"Walker, please! I don't want to get involved in this. I didn't sign up for any of this!" Dr. Shimba's voice cracked, revealing the fear he had kept bottled inside.

"I understand, but you're already in this. Just do as I say," Walker said, his tone firm. "We'll figure it out. Just hold tight."

He ended the call, adrenaline surging through his veins. "We need to move. Dr. Shimba is in danger. That package could be a threat — or a lure."

Martinez nodded, already gathering her gear. "We can't take any chances. He might be the key to unraveling this entire operation."

They rushed out of the precinct, the weight of their mission heavy in the air. Walker's mind spun with the implications of what Dr. Shimba had just said. The black SUV — was it linked to Lynch, or was it another player in this deadly game?

As they raced through the bustling streets of New York, Walker couldn't shake the feeling that time was running out. They had to get to Dr. Shimba before the situation escalated further.

Arriving at Dr. Shimba's office building, they parked a block away, scanning the street for the telltale black SUV. "There it is!" Martinez pointed as they spotted the vehicle parked inconspicuously across the street, its dark windows concealing the occupants within.

"Let's approach cautiously," Walker instructed. "We don't know who's inside or what they're capable of."

They moved stealthily, staying close to the buildings and blending into the crowd as they approached the office. The entrance loomed ahead, its glass doors reflecting the late afternoon sun. Walker's heart raced as he pushed through the door, stepping into the lobby.

"Stay here. I'll check on Shimba," Walker said, motioning for Martinez to cover him. He nodded at the reception desk, where a nervous attendant watched him with wide eyes.

Walker dashed to the elevator, pressing the button for Dr. Shimba's floor. The elevator dinged, and the doors slid open. He stepped into the corridor, glancing at the office doors. As he approached Dr. Shimba's office, he noticed it was ajar. The hairs on the back of his neck stood up.

"Dr. Shimba?" he called out, pushing the door open cautiously. Inside, the office was in disarray — papers scattered, a chair overturned. The only thing that seemed untouched was the ominous black box, sitting in the center of the room.

"Dr. Shimba!" Walker called again, his voice echoing in the silence. Panic surged through him as he moved further inside, eyes scanning for any sign of the curator.

"Walker!" Martinez's voice rang out behind him, and he turned to see her rushing into the office, her expression grave. "What happened?"

"It looks like he was here, but he's gone now," Walker replied, his gaze locked on the box. "We need to open that."

Martinez glanced at the door, her instincts on high alert. "Are you sure? It could be a trap."

"We have to know what we're dealing with. If he's in danger, we might find a clue here," Walker insisted, stepping closer to the box.

He knelt beside it, noticing the intricate designs etched into the surface, symbols that sent a chill down his spine. With a deep breath, he lifted the lid, heart pounding as he prepared for the worst.

Inside lay a collection of carefully arranged documents and a single, ominous envelope sealed with red wax. Walker pulled out the envelope, noticing a familiar emblem stamped into the wax — a symbol he had seen before, tied to the very criminal organization they had been tracking.

"This isn't good," he muttered, breaking the seal. Inside was a note, written in elegant cursive, that sent a shiver down his spine: "You should have stayed out of this, Detective. The next move is ours."

Martinez leaned in, reading over his shoulder. "This is a threat, and it's aimed directly at you."

"We have to find Dr. Shimba," Walker said, determination hardening in his gut. "If they've taken him, we need to find out where."

Suddenly, the sound of a door slamming echoed down the hallway. Walker and Martinez exchanged a glance, adrenaline surging through them as they both reached for their weapons.

"Did you hear that?" Martinez whispered, her eyes scanning the corridor.

"Yeah. We need to move, now!" Walker said, backing toward the office door, his heart racing.

But before they could make their exit, a group of masked men burst into the office, weapons drawn and faces obscured. Walker and Martinez immediately took defensive stances, prepared to fight for their lives.

"Get down!" Martinez shouted, but the intruders were already closing in, their intentions clear — they wanted the box, and they weren't leaving without it.

In that moment, everything changed. Walker realized they were not just facing petty criminals; they were now entangled in a web of danger that reached far beyond what they had ever imagined. And as they prepared to defend themselves, he couldn't help but wonder: how deep did this conspiracy go, and who else was involved?

# CHAPTER 14

## THE HUNT BEGINS

Detective Walker paced the precinct, the rhythmic clicking of his shoes cutting through the tense silence. Dr. Shimba had disappeared without a trace, his phone going silent minutes after their last frantic call. It was as if he had vanished into thin air, leaving only the mysterious black box and an unsettling trail of questions in his wake.

Martinez entered the room, her face a mix of concern and frustration. "Nothing. We've got no security footage, no witnesses who saw him leave. It's as if someone wiped the entire scene clean."

Walker clenched his jaw, feeling the weight of time slipping away. "Whoever did this had resources. They're covering their tracks at every turn."

"Do you think he was taken?" Martinez asked, voicing the fear that had been gnawing at both of them.

Walker sighed, leaning against the wall, his mind racing. "It's possible. Or worse — he might have been coerced. Dr. Shimba was terrified when he called, and now we've got no way to reach him." He rubbed his forehead, trying to focus. "We need to start with what we do have. That box in his office and that threat. Whoever's behind this doesn't want us investigating."

Martinez nodded, her fingers tapping the edge of the table. "Maybe we can trace the SUV. There was something about it, Walker. An aura of precision and professionalism — it didn't feel random."

"Good idea. Run a search on every black SUV spotted around the Diamond District over the last few days. Let's see if it turns up a rental or a pattern of sightings near key locations," Walker replied, his determination sharpening.

They worked quickly, sifting through hours of traffic footage and vehicle registration databases. The minutes ticked by, turning into hours, but finally, a lead emerged.

"Here!" Martinez exclaimed, pointing at the screen. "This SUV. It matches the description, and it's been seen in three separate locations near the Diamond District. Look at the timing — it shows up within minutes of each of those diamond shipments you flagged as unusual."

Walker studied the footage closely, noting the SUV's license plate. "Bingo. This is more than just surveillance. They're shadowing Shimba's deliveries."

"But why target him?" Martinez mused, looking puzzled. "Dr. Shimba's just a curator. He's no smuggler or dealer. His only connection is that he received that diamond package from overseas."

"Exactly. That package — it's the common thread. Whatever's inside it, someone is willing to go to extreme lengths to keep it under wraps," Walker said, his mind piecing together fragments of the case. "We need to find out where it came from and who sent it to him."

They reached out to customs and managed to obtain records of Dr. Shimba's package. The sender's name was unfamiliar, but the address listed a location in a remote, isolated part of Africa — a region known for illegal mining operations and underground diamond deals.

"This sender's no ordinary business," Martinez observed, her voice wary. "We might be dealing with international smugglers or traffickers."

"It could explain why Dr. Shimba was pulled into this," Walker replied. "He might have unwittingly become a courier for something far more valuable — and dangerous — than he realized."

Just then, a call came in on the precinct's mainline, breaking their focus. Walker picked it up, his instincts tingling. "Detective Walker."

A distorted voice responded, low and threatening. "You're playing a dangerous game, Detective. Dr. Shimba is under our protection now. If you value his life, you'll back off."

Walker tightened his grip on the phone, anger simmering beneath his calm facade. "If you harm him, there won't be a place on earth you can hide from us."

The caller chuckled darkly. "This isn't a negotiation. You have one last chance — walk away, or suffer the consequences."

The line went dead, leaving a cold silence in its wake. Martinez looked at him, her face tense. "What did they say?"

"They have him. They're warning us to back off," Walker said, setting the phone down with a grim expression. "But they just made one fatal mistake — now we know he's alive, and that means we can find him."

Martinez nodded, determination hardening her gaze. "Let's turn this around. If they're so determined to get us off the case, then we'll do the opposite. We'll dig deeper than ever."

They spent the next few hours mobilizing resources, calling in favors, and coordinating with other law enforcement agencies. Every clue, every minor lead, every possible connection to Dr. Shimba's case was pursued relentlessly.

Finally, they came across a breakthrough. Martinez pulled up a photo taken near one of the diamond exchanges Dr. Shimba had frequented. In the background, almost hidden in shadow, was the face of someone they had seen before: a known broker with ties to smuggling rings.

"This broker, Peter Lang," Walker said, squinting at the photo. "He's on every watchlist in the book, yet somehow he's been under the radar for years."

Martinez nodded. "Lang's reputation is infamous in underground circles. If he's involved, it means that the stakes are even higher than we thought."

As they began building a profile on Lang, Walker's phone buzzed with a message. It was from an unknown number, a simple text: "You're closer than you think. But be careful — the closer you get, the darker it becomes."

Walker looked up at Martinez, the cryptic message weighing heavily on him. "This is more than just diamonds,

Sarah. Whatever Dr. Shimba got himself into, it's bigger than we ever imagined."

She met his gaze, the determination in her eyes unwavering. "Then let's get ready for the fight of our lives. Because we're not backing down until we bring him home."

# CHAPTER 15

## INTO THE ABYSS

Detective Walker and Detective Martinez prepared for the final showdown, knowing that everything they had worked for — every lead, every late night, every threat — had come down to this moment. Their investigation had led them to a secluded warehouse on the outskirts of the city, where Peter Lang was rumored to operate his underground dealings. The tension was thick, the kind that signaled either victory or utter defeat.

They arrived at the warehouse in the dead of night, their footsteps muffled by the gravel underfoot. The warehouse was dark, looming like a silent predator against the city skyline. Its few broken windows and boarded-up doors gave no indication of the hive of illicit activities hidden within. Walker's hand hovered over his holstered gun, every muscle tense and ready.

Martinez pointed to a side door. "That's our way in. Surveillance confirms Lang and his men use it as a secondary entrance for their high-profile 'clients.' If Dr. Shimba's here, that's where they'll bring him."

They slipped through the side door, the interior of the warehouse vast and filled with metal crates, towering shadows, and echoes that seemed to stretch endlessly. They moved silently, communicating in hand signals, their senses heightened by the charged atmosphere.

Just as they approached a cluster of crates, they heard voices echoing from an adjacent room. Walker motioned to Martinez, and they crept closer, peering through a narrow gap in the crates. Inside, they saw Peter Lang himself, calm and composed, his sharp gaze fixed on Dr. Shimba, who was bound to a chair, looking battered but defiant.

Lang's voice cut through the silence. "Dr. Shimba, you've been remarkably resilient, I'll give you that. But your time is running out. The package you received was never meant to leave Africa. It contains something… invaluable. And now, because of your ignorance, we're all at risk."

Dr. Shimba, though visibly shaken, looked Lang directly in the eyes. "Whatever it is, I had no part in your schemes. I was just trying to do my job. You'll never get away with this."

Lang chuckled, the sound chillingly smooth. "Oh, I don't plan to 'get away with' anything. I own the authorities, the system, even the people you trusted to help you. They all report to me in one way or another. And you, my friend, are a loose end that needs to be tied up."

Walker clenched his fists, his anger rising. Martinez gave him a steady look, reminding him to wait for the right moment. They couldn't risk an impulsive move — not when Dr. Shimba's life hung in the balance.

Suddenly, Lang's phone buzzed, and his expression changed as he glanced at the message. His tone turned cold, his gaze shifting back to Dr. Shimba. "It seems our guests have arrived early. They're eager to retrieve the item personally. As for you, Dr. Shimba… this is where we part ways."

Walker gave Martinez a nod, and they sprang into action. Martinez kicked open the door, her gun aimed squarely at Lang, while Walker took cover, shouting, "NYPD! Hands up!"

Lang's men scrambled, reaching for weapons, but Walker and Martinez were faster. A shot rang out as one of Lang's henchmen lunged forward, and he crumpled to the ground. Lang, however, simply raised his hands, a calm, calculated smile on his face.

"You think this is over, detectives?" Lang said, his voice steady. "You're just scratching the surface. The network I work for is bigger than anything you can comprehend. And you — you're nothing more than a minor inconvenience."

Walker ignored him, moving quickly to free Dr. Shimba from his bindings. The professor looked weak but managed a grateful nod. "I thought... I thought it was the end," he murmured.

"We're not letting them take you, Dr. Shimba," Walker replied, his voice firm.

Just as they began moving Dr. Shimba toward the exit, a flashbang detonated, filling the room with blinding light and deafening noise. Walker instinctively shielded Dr. Shimba, and the world spun as chaos erupted around them. Through the haze, he could see dark-clad figures storming into the warehouse — an elite team, far too organized to be regular criminals. They moved with precision, their sole purpose to retrieve the mysterious package.

Martinez fired off a shot, but the figures seemed undeterred, forcing her and Walker to retreat deeper into the shadows with Dr. Shimba in tow. They maneuvered through the maze of crates, dodging their pursuers, their breaths coming in short, tense gasps.

"Who… who are they?" Dr. Shimba asked, his voice barely audible over the sound of footsteps.

"Whoever they are, they're the ones Lang was expecting. We need to get you out of here — fast," Walker replied, glancing around for an escape route.

They spotted a narrow stairwell leading to the roof and took it, climbing rapidly, desperate to put as much distance as possible between them and their attackers. On the roof, the night air was sharp, and the city lights spread out before them, an almost surreal contrast to the danger they were in.

But the elite team was relentless, appearing at the rooftop entrance within moments. Walker and Martinez exchanged a quick look, their determination unbroken. They took defensive positions, ready to make a stand.

Then, as if on cue, sirens wailed from below. Backup had arrived — the NYPD had been tracking their movements. Squad cars surrounded the building, and more officers stormed into the warehouse, forcing Lang's operatives to retreat.

As the officers secured the scene, Walker and Martinez finally allowed themselves a sigh of relief. The danger was over — for now.

Dr. Shimba, shaken but safe, looked at them with a mix of gratitude and fear. "Thank you… I owe you my life. But I don't think this is the end, is it?"

Walker nodded slowly. "No, Dr. Shimba. Whatever's inside that package, it's connected to something much bigger. We've only begun to unravel the truth."

As they descended from the rooftop, the magnitude of their discovery settled in. The case wasn't over. It was only the beginning of a larger conspiracy, one that would take them deeper into the shadows than they had ever ventured before.

And for Detective Walker and Detective Martinez, the hunt was just beginning.

# CHAPTER 16

**THE CALL FROM THE ABYSS**

As Detective Walker and Detective Martinez hurried Dr. Shimba down the stairwell, the tension in the air was palpable. Their hearts raced, adrenaline coursing through their veins as they pushed through the door onto the ground floor. They barely made it outside when Walker's phone buzzed urgently in his pocket. He glanced at the screen — it was Lieutenant Lois Mesh. The gravity of the moment was not lost on him; when Mesh called, it was rarely good news.

"Hold on a second," Walker said, raising a hand to Martinez. She nodded, keeping an eye out for any lingering threats. He stepped aside and answered the call, trying to mask the rising anxiety in his voice. "Lieutenant Mesh, what's going on?"

"Walker," Mesh's voice came through the line, strained and sharp. "I need you to listen carefully. We've had a development back at the precinct. It's not just the diamond heist. We've got a major situation unfolding, and it ties back to your case."

"What do you mean?" Walker asked, his pulse quickening. "What's happened?"

"There's been a leak — a snitch within the department," Mesh said, her voice dropping to a whisper, as if the walls themselves might be listening. "A few of our officers have been working with Lang and his crew. They knew about the stakeout and the backup we sent to you. This whole operation has been compromised from the inside."

Walker felt the weight of her words settle in his stomach like a stone. "So you're telling me that someone in our own precinct has been feeding information to the enemy? That's why they were so organized tonight?"

"Exactly. We're running a full investigation now, but I need you and Martinez to stay on high alert. If Lang's people are involved, they'll be looking for you. They'll want to tie up loose ends, and you just rescued a key player in their scheme."

The chill that ran down Walker's spine was nothing compared to the anger that surged within him. "How deep does this go, Lieutenant? How many officers are involved?"

"I can't say for sure yet, but I'm sending over a team to assist you. They'll be discreet, but you can't trust anyone right now, not even the guys in uniform," Mesh cautioned. "I need you to secure Dr. Shimba and get him to a safe location immediately. I'll arrange for protection."

"What about you? Are you safe?" Walker asked, concern edging into his voice.

"I'm fine for now, but I have to get back to the precinct. We'll talk more when I have more information. Just be careful, Walker. I have a feeling they'll come after you next."

The line went dead, leaving Walker standing there, the weight of the revelation settling heavily on his shoulders. He turned to Martinez, who was still watching the surroundings with a vigilant eye. "We've got a serious problem," he said, his voice low and intense.

"What is it?" she asked, stepping closer.

"There's a mole in the precinct," Walker replied, the anger palpable in his tone. "They've been feeding information to Lang and his crew. That's why they were so well-prepared tonight. And now, we can't trust anyone — not even our backup."

Martinez's eyes widened, the realization sinking in. "So, this goes deeper than we thought. We need to get Dr. Shimba to safety before they come for him again."

"Right," Walker said, glancing back at Dr. Shimba, who was leaning against a nearby car, looking pale but resolute. "We need to move. We can't stay here. The precinct is compromised."

As they quickly ushered Dr. Shimba into the backseat of an unmarked car, Walker felt the air shift around them. The night was filled with tension, a heavy silence that pressed in on them as they pulled away from the warehouse. With every turn they took, every streetlight that flickered past, the looming threat of betrayal felt ever closer.

"Where are we heading?" Martinez asked, her voice steady despite the chaos swirling around them.

"There's a safe house we can use. I trust the officer there," Walker replied, but as the words left his mouth, he felt a gnawing doubt. Who could they trust anymore?

Just then, a shadow loomed in the rearview mirror. Walker's heart raced as he spotted a black SUV tailing them, its headlights piercing the darkness like a predator stalking its prey. "We've got company," he warned, gripping the wheel tighter as he accelerated.

"Can you lose them?" Martinez asked, her eyes darting back and forth between the road and the looming threat behind them.

"I'm going to try," Walker replied, a fierce determination fueling his actions. He took a sharp turn down an alley, hoping to shake off their pursuers. The car screeched as they navigated the narrow streets, their hearts pounding in unison.

But the SUV was relentless, weaving through traffic with ease. The tension mounted as Walker glanced at Martinez, her expression a mix of fear and focus. Dr. Shimba, too, was on edge, his fingers gripping the seat as he whispered a silent prayer.

"Get ready," Walker said, feeling the weight of responsibility. "If they catch up to us, we need to be ready for anything."

Just as he finished speaking, a shot rang out, shattering the silence of the night. The bullet struck the rear window, sending shards of glass raining down. "Go, go, go!" Martinez shouted, her voice cutting through the chaos.

Walker pushed the pedal to the floor, heart racing as he maneuvered through the tight streets. They needed to find a way to escape this trap, to get Dr. Shimba to safety before it was too late. With danger closing in, they were thrust deeper into a web of deception, where trust was a rare commodity and every decision could be their last.

In the shadows, the real battle was just beginning.

# CONCLUSION

Conclusion of Volume II: Shadows Within

The SUV continued its relentless pursuit through the darkened streets of New York. Walker's knuckles were white as he gripped the wheel, the car swerving between traffic with desperate precision. Martinez kept her gun drawn, eyes darting between the rearview mirror and the windows. Dr. Shimba sat silent in the backseat, his face pale and eyes wide with a fear he couldn't conceal.

With another sharp turn, Walker maneuvered the car into an unmarked alleyway, hidden between two towering buildings. He switched off the headlights and held his breath as the black SUV roared past, unaware that its prey had slipped into the shadows. The city hummed around them, oblivious to the chase, as the echoes of tires on asphalt faded into the distance.

"Everyone alright?" Walker asked, his voice low but firm.

Dr. Shimba nodded, still shaken. "I don't know how much longer I can handle this. Who are these people, Detective?"

"It's worse than we thought, Doctor," Martinez replied grimly. "There's someone on the inside feeding them everything they need to know. They're not just after the diamonds; they're after control. And right now, they're one step ahead of us."

As they drove toward the safe house in silence, Walker's mind was racing. Mesh's revelation of a mole within their own ranks loomed heavily, reshaping everything he thought he understood about the case. Who could he trust in a precinct riddled with betrayal?

The car pulled into the driveway of a secluded building on the outskirts of the city. Walker stepped out, scanning the area before opening the back door for Dr. Shimba and guiding him inside. They locked the doors behind them, and Walker exhaled deeply, feeling a momentary sense of relief.

"I'll check the perimeter," Martinez said, already moving to the windows, her eyes sharp with vigilance.

Walker turned to Dr. Shimba, whose face reflected a complex mixture of terror and determination. "Doctor, I need you to tell us everything about these diamonds — not just where they came from, but why they're worth dying for."

Dr. Shimba hesitated, then lowered his voice. "They're not just ordinary diamonds, Detective. They contain… information. Encoded data that could expose an international network — a syndicate so powerful it reaches into law enforcement, politics, and beyond. This data could ruin them, bring their entire empire crashing down. And they know it."

Walker and Martinez exchanged a look of stunned realization. They had stumbled into something far larger than they had anticipated. The diamonds were more than just jewels — they were a threat, a weapon that could bring down the most dangerous criminal organization the city had ever seen.

Just then, Walker's phone buzzed, and he saw Lieutenant Mesh's name flash across the screen. He answered, holding his breath as he braced for more bad news.

"Walker," Mesh's voice was barely a whisper, and he could hear the strain in her tone. "You need to know… there's more to this than the syndicate. We've traced a connection overseas — and it's tied directly to something far larger than we thought. They're after more than just the diamonds. They're trying to secure every piece of information that could link back to them. It's global, Walker. And it's coming for us."

The line went dead, leaving only the faint hum of static. Walker stared at his phone, a chill running through him. If what Mesh said was true, they were now tangled in the center of a conspiracy that reached beyond New York's borders — a web of secrets, betrayal, and violence with no visible end.

Dr. Shimba met his gaze, understanding dawning in his eyes. "Detective… if you're going to keep me safe, you're going to need more than just protection. You're going to need allies. Powerful ones."

Walker nodded, feeling the weight of Dr. Shimba's words. "We're going to need all the help we can get."

The room fell silent as each of them absorbed the magnitude of the battle they were now part of, their lives intertwined with forces they could barely comprehend.

Introduction to Volume III: The Web Unveiled

As Walker, Martinez, and Dr. Shimba settled into their temporary safe haven, the realization dawned that they had merely scratched the surface. Every lead they had followed, every piece of evidence gathered, had led them closer to an unimaginable truth. The syndicate, once a local operation, was part of an elaborate network stretching across continents.

In Volume III: The Web Unveiled, Walker and Martinez will confront this sprawling empire, uncovering the network of alliances, betrayals, and global corruption that lurks behind every corner. The mole in their precinct, the encrypted diamonds, and the chase through the streets of New York were just the beginning. Now, the true players will emerge from the shadows.

Their enemies will grow bolder, their allies scarce, and the stakes higher than ever as they unravel the web of deceit. But with every step they take, the question looms larger: who, in a city of secrets, can they truly trust?